This igloo book belongs to:

....

Published in 2021
First published in the UK by Igloo Books Ltd
An imprint of Igloo Books Ltd
Cottage Farm, NN6 0BJ, UK
Owned by Bonnier Books
Sveavägen 56, Stockholm, Sweden
www.igloobooks.com

0821 001 PK
10 12 13 11 9
ISBN: 978-1-78197-838-2

Written by Melanie Joyce

Illustrated by Annabel Spencely

Printed and manufactured in China

Christmas Magic

igloobooks

I'm bursting to tell you about Christmas and why it's so much fun.

It's the sparkliest, jingliest time of year and I can't wait for it to come.

Daddy will get the Christmas tree and put it up in the hall.

I'll cover it with fairy lights and sparkly glittering balls.

I'll write my note to Santa, but I always change my mind.

I'm sure Santa won't be cross though. I think he's very kind.

Carol singers will ring the bell and sing outside our door.

When they've sung their songs, I'll ask, "Can you sing some more?"

There'll be Christmas cards to all my friends, stuck with glitter and glue.

Look out when the postman comes, there might be one for you!

I'll throw snowballs at my brother, they'll go whoosh and thud and splat!

We'll laugh and make a snowman and he'll wear my Daddy's hat.

Mum will read me stories and tell tales of Christmas past.

Then when the fire goes out, it will be time for bed at last.

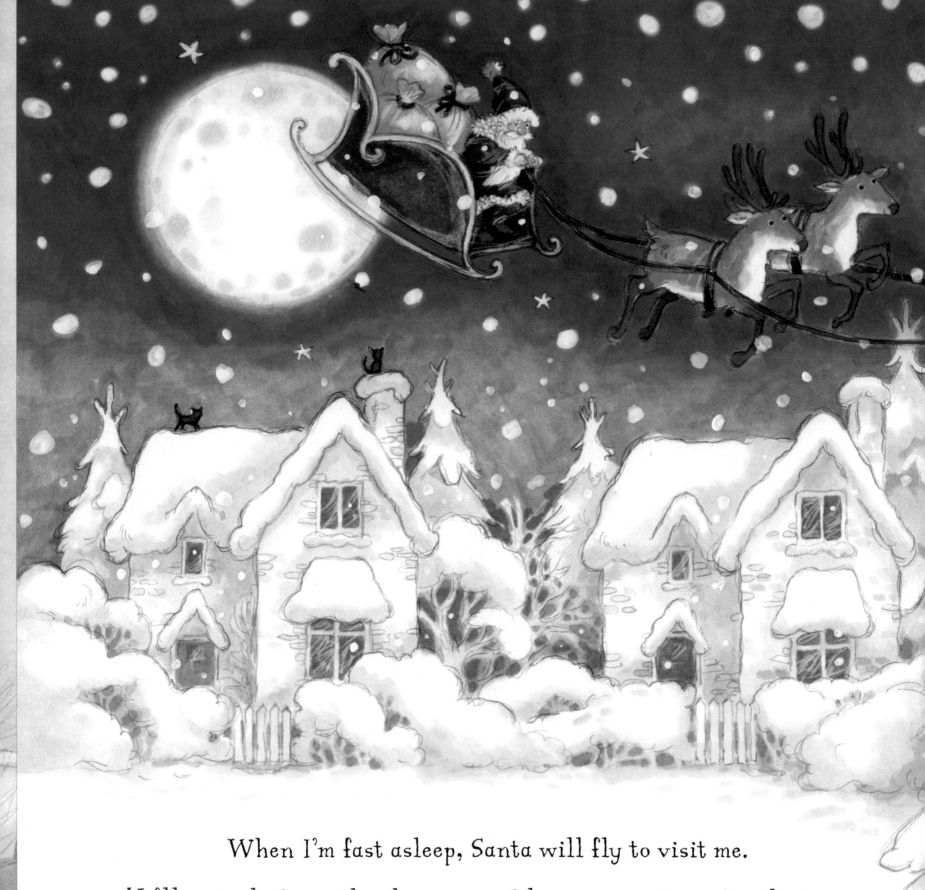

When I'm fast asleep, Santa will fly to visit me.

He'll wriggle down the chimney and leave presents under the tree.

I won't sleep because I'll be so excited. Christmas is loads of fun.

In the morning, I'll run downstairs and shout, "Merry Christmas, everyone!"

Happy Christmas!